KU-033-115

Daljit and the Unqualified Wizard

CATHERINE STORR

Illustrated by
TONI GOFFE

HEINEMANN · LONDON

William Heinemann Ltd
Michelin House, 81 Fulham Road,
London SW3 6RB

LONDON MELBOURNE AUCKLAND

First published 1989
Text © 1989 Catherine Storr
Illustrations © 1989 Toni Goffe

ISBN 0 434 93057 1
Printed in Hong Kong by
Mandarin Offset

A school pack of SUPERCHAMPS 1–6
is available from
Heinemann Educational Books
ISBN 0 435 00090 X

Chapter One

'AT YOUR AGE, you should be able to read. Both of you,' Daljit's and Ben's teacher said.

'I can read TOILETS. And LADIES and GENTLEMEN. And EXIT,' Daljit said.

'That won't get you far,' Mr Smith said, disagreeably. He was often disagreeable.

'Yes it does. It means I don't go into the LADIES' toilets.'

'I can read NO ENTRY and MEN AT WORK, so I can tell my Dad not to drive up one way streets,' Ben said.

'You should be able to read Books,' Mr Smith said. He pronounced the word *Books* as if it was a holy word, like *God* or *Poetry*. 'If you can't read Books, you will never pass your exams.'

'My Dad hasn't passed any exams,'
Ben said.

Mr Smith didn't know what to say to
this. He couldn't very well tell Ben that
his Dad was a no-good idjut. 'But your
Dad would be pleased if you passed your
exams. And so would yours, Daljit,' he
said at last.

'Why are exams always about books?
Why can't I pass an exam in football?
Or music?' Daljit wondered. But he did
not say this to Mr Smith. Instead he
agreed that perhaps his Dad would be
pleased if he learned to read books as
well as useful signs and notices – though
really it was his Mum who made more
fuss about it.

'My aunt Sarry's going to teach me at
weekends. She's got a special way of
teaching, and she says I'll be able to read

properly real quick,' Ben said.

'You mean soon. Yes. Your Mum was telling me. But does she know how to teach?' Mr Smith asked.

' 'Course she does. She's a teacher at a proper big school. Not for little kids like this,' Ben said.

Mr Smith looked as if he did not like this.

'Schools for younger pupils are just as important as schools for older children, Ben. We'll have to see how you get on. Have you got one of these clever aunts, Daljit? No? Then you'll have to go to a Tutor. Twice a week for special lessons,' Mr Smith said.

'What's a Tutor?' Daljit asked.

'Someone whose job it is to teach stupid boys, one at a time, who don't want to learn in class,' Mr Smith said, nastily.

Daljit's Tutor was called Mr Jones. 'He'll see that you learn to read really quickly,' Mr Smith said.

'You mean all in a minute? Like magic?' Daljit asked.

'Don't talk so stupid. There's no such thing as magic,' Mr Smith said, slamming down a pile of unfortunate Books on his desk.

Chapter Two

DALJIT DID NOT want to go for lessons
from a Tutor. He thought that anyone
called Mr Jones would probably be as
dull and as aggravating as Mr Smith.
His lessons were to be after school, too,
which meant missing football on
Wednesdays. The first afternoon when
he had to go to see Mr Jones, he walked

very slowly along the road where Mr Jones lived. He felt stupid. He was sure that Mr Jones would ask him to read out of a book and all the letters on the page would turn into clumps of squiggles that didn't mean anything, and he would feel stupider still.

When he reached the door of 81 Elder Grove, he felt as miserable as he ever had in all his life. However, he rang the bell, and when the door opened, he saw Mr Jones.

The first thing Daljit noticed was that Mr Jones was not at all like Mr Smith. Mr Smith was quite old, but he liked to think that he was quite young. He wore patched jeans and scruffy pullovers, and combed his three hairs right across his head, pretending that the shiny bald skin didn't show through. Once he had started to grow a beard, but as soon as he saw that parts of it were going to be grey, he had shaved it off very quickly.

Mr Jones was also oldish. But he was not pretending to be anything else. He was short and stout, a comfortable, solid shape. His hair was cut short all over his head, so that it stood up like prickly, grey-brown grass. He wore a blue boiler suit.

'Is it Daljit? Come in,' he said, and shook Daljit by the hand. Mr Jones's hand was warm and dry and quick. Mr Smith didn't shake hands with his pupils very often, and when he did his hand was damp, and curiously flabby.

Daljit followed Mr Jones along a passage into a big room. There was a large table, a cooker, shelves of different coloured bottles and more books than Daljit had ever seen. They did not make him feel any happier.

'Sit down. What am I supposed to be teaching you? Is it numbers? Or is it history? Greek? Or is it spells?'

Spells? Daljit hated spelling lessons even more than reading. He was hopeless at spelling. He said quickly, 'It's reading.'

'Reading what, boy? Reading the stars? The future? The Scriptures? What do you want to read?'

'Just ordinary reading. Books,' Daljit said. He would much rather learn how to read the stars, but he didn't think that Mr Smith, or his Mum either, would approve.

'Books. Yes. Welsh books?' Mr Jones asked hopefully.

'Not Welsh. English.'

'English books. Yes. Of course. We'll start right away,' Mr Jones said. He looked along one of the shelves and brought a pile of cards to the table. He put one in front of Daljit. Daljit saw a sentence printed on it in large clear letters.

'Can you read that?' Mr Jones asked.

Daljit could. *The Hat sat on the Cat. But that isn't right! It ought to be, The Cat sat on the Mat,'* he said.

'So boring. Try this one,' Mr Jones said, putting another card on the table. Daljit read:

The rat sat
on the hat
Pat has a
tat bat
Rat-a-tat
tat.

'It's different from what we have to read at school,' he said.

'So I should hope. Try this one,' Mr Jones said, and he put another card on the table. Daljit found this more difficult. He got as far as *See, mother*, but then he had to have help. The whole card read, *See, mother, Rover has a bone. The bone has bitten Rover.*

'Could a bone bite a dog?' he asked.

'Why not, if it has teeth?' Mr Jones said. He said a word which Daljit couldn't hear, and there, suddenly, on the card, was the picture of a human skull, with two rows of excellent, grinning teeth. The picture disappeared again so quickly that Daljit wondered whether he had really seen it, or just imagined it.

'How did you do that? Is it like magic painting books?' he asked.

'Certainly not. That's for babies. Not real magic at all,' Mr Jones said.

'What is real magic? You mean, like card tricks?'

'That's prestidigitation.'

'What?' Daljit said, not understanding.

'Conjuring. The quickness of the hand deceives the eye.'

'I saw a real magician once. He sawed a lady in half. In a box. Well, it looked as if he did. Only when she came out of the box, she was all in one piece again.'

'They call themselves magicians. Really, they're just clever with their hands. And, boy, how they talk! They can't cast spells,' Mr Jones said.

'Can *you* cast spells?' Daljit asked.

Mr Jones put another card on the table. There were a lot of long words on it. The only one that Daljit could read, was an *and* in the middle. 'I can't read that!' he said.

Mr Jones pointed a stubby finger at him and whispered something. Then he said, 'Now try!'

Daljit looked at the card again and, to his surprise, he read out, *'Alligators and crocodiles are mutually antagonistic.'*

'What does that mean?' he asked.

'You know what a *crocodile* is?'

'I know what *alligators* are, too. It's the other words I don't understand.'

'*Mutually* means they both feel the same. *Antagonistic* means they don't like each other.'

'But I read it!' Daljit said. He looked at the card again, and now he couldn't read it at all. Except, of course, that he knew what it said, so the word *crocodiles* looked somehow familiar.

'How did I read it just now?' he asked,

puzzled.

'Magic.'

'Could you magic me to read anything?' Daljit imagined himself in school the next day, reading everything straight off. That would surprise Mr Smith all right, and he'd have beaten Ben. But he didn't really want to beat Ben all that much. Ben was his friend.

'Anything you like,' Mr Jones said.

'Then I wouldn't have to come here twice a week, would I? Won't you do it now? Please!'

'It isn't quite as easy as that–' Mr Jones said, and then stopped.

'But if you can do real magic!' Daljit tried to persuade him.

'I can. In a way. But . . .'

'I *saw* you do magic. You made me read about the crocodiles.'

'You see, it's like this.' Mr Jones stopped again. Then he went on, 'I went to the Imperial College of Spells and Magic. I was there for years. I was one of their best pupils. It all came easy to me. But in the end . . . I never qualified.'

'What's that mean?' Daljit asked.

'I didn't pass the exams. I don't know what happened. It was in what's called Practical Magic. You have to cast spells in front of your examiners. It should have been child's play, but I got cold feet. Couldn't do the simplest thing. They asked me to turn a mouse into an elephant, something I'd done plenty of times when I was practising. I made a stupid mistake.'

'What happened?'

'I turned the mouse into a tiger – and before I could stop it, it ate one of the

18

examiners. So they failed me. You can't really blame them.' Mr Jones looked so sad that Daljit wanted to cheer him up.

'But you can still do magic.'

'I can do some magic, but it's uncertain.'

'How do you mean?' Daljit asked.

'You see, I wasn't allowed to stay at the College for my last year. So there were things I never learned properly. Like timing.'

'Timing?' Daljit said, not understanding.

'I never know how long my spells are going to last. They work all right when I do them and then . . . they sort of wear off. Like your reading that card about crocodiles. Or sometimes they last longer than they should. Much longer. That can be even worse.'

'I wish my reading had lasted longer

than it should.'

'Sometimes it's awkward. For instance, this morning I thought I'd see if I remembered how to turn my pencil into a snake.'

'*Did* you remember?' Daljit asked.

'And now I don't know how to turn it back again. And I need a pencil, and I

don't need a snake. Not just at present.'

'Do you mean there's a snake here? In this room? A real live snake?' Daljit asked, a little nervous.

'Under the saucer on the sideboard,' Mr Jones said. He added, 'Go and look if you don't believe me.'

Daljit did not fancy picking up a

saucer with a real live snake under it. But he did not want Mr Jones to think he was a coward. He went to the sideboard and tilted the saucer a very little. Nothing happened. He tilted it a little further and saw a slim straight shape, lying quite still. Feeling braver, he picked the saucer right up and saw a perfectly ordinary pencil. He was relieved, but also a little disappointed.

'Was it a poisonous snake?' he asked.

'I've no idea. Now, that's the end of your lesson for today. See you on Friday,' said Mr Jones. He showed Daljit out, very politely, shaking hands with him again at the front door.

'How did you get on with your tutor?' Daljit's Mum asked when he got home.

'He's all right. He's a lot all righter than Mr Smith.'

'What did you read today?' his Mum asked.

'About cats. And rats and mats. And crocodiles,' Daljit said.

'Crocodiles! You must be getting on fast,' his Mum said, pleased.

In school the next day, Ben asked Daljit how his first lesson with Mr Jones had gone.

'It wasn't bad,' Daljit said. He didn't want to tell Ben yet about Mr Jones being a failed wizard.

'Is he going to teach you to read real quick? I bet my aunt Sarry'll teach me a lot quicker than your Mr Jones,' Ben said.

'I bet she won't,' Daljit said, but he did not feel at all sure about this.

Chapter Three

ON FRIDAY, DALJIT walked quickly along
Elder Grove. Having a wizard, even an
unqualified wizard, for a teacher, was
interesting, he decided. After they had
shaken hands at the door, he sat down at
Mr Jones' table, hoping for some
exciting surprise.

'Here's the first card,' Mr Jones said.

Daljit read it out.

'No milk today, thank you.'

'That's a mistake. Not your reading,
but the card. I meant to leave it outside

the door for the milkman,' Mr Jones
said, searching for another card.

'Won't you do some magic first?'
Daljit asked.

'Your school is paying me to teach
you to read, not to do magic,' Mr Jones
said, and for a moment he sounded
almost like Mr Smith. 'Here. Read this,'
he said.

This was much more difficult. Daljit
began to spell it out. *'When the moon is
full, take three loaves . . .'*

'Leaves,' said Mr Jones sharply.

'*Take three leaves of . . .*' Then came a tremendously long word, which he couldn't make out at all.

'Let me see. Ah! I wondered where I'd put that spell,' Mr Jones said, taking the card and reading it himself.

'What sort of a spell is it?' Daljit asked.

'Turns someone into a hedgehog. Or a hedgehog into something else, I'm not quite sure which way round it goes. Let me see. Full moon . . . yes. That's next Monday or Tuesday. What a happy coincidence! And three leaves of . . . Yes. Good. I'm glad to have that back,' Mr Jones said, putting the card in his pocket.

'What's that mean?' Daljit asked.

'What does what mean?'

'That word you said. Co – something.'

'Coincidence. Means two things happening at the same time. Or nearly the same. I mean, you finding this spell today, so that I'll just have time to get what I need for it before next Tuesday.'

'Can I see you do it?' Daljit asked.

'I don't see why not.' Mr Jones consulted a large calendar, hanging on the wall. 'Could you get here at seventeen minutes past four o'clock? That's the precise moment when the moon is at her fullest.'

'I suppose I could if I came straight on from school. We get out at half past three on Tuesday afternoons,' Daljit said.

'Not the afternoon, boy. Morning. Seventeen minutes past four o'clock in the morning. Will you be coming here then?'

Daljit knew that his Mum would have a fit if he left the house at four o'clock in the morning for any reason. She would have twenty fits if she thought that he'd gone to see a person turn into a hedgehog. So he said, politely, 'No, I'm afraid I can't,' after which Mr Jones became very serious and made Daljit read the proper reading cards.

This might have been boring, if the sentences on the cards had not been so very different from those which Daljit had seen before in school. On the first, he read, *Fish can fly, but can flies fish?*

When he had managed to read it all, the card suddenly showed him the picture of several flies in paper boats on a small pool, fishing for dear life with rod and line. The next card, which Mr Jones had to help with, had on it, *Beware of the masquerading*

mushroom. 'What's *masquerading*?' Daljit asked.

'In disguise. Pretending to be something it isn't. This mushroom is pretending to be a quite ordinary field mushroom, and really it's extremely poisonous and if you ate it, you would be very ill.' Mr Jones touched the card with a stubby finger, and Daljit saw the picture of a large mushroom, brown on top, creamy white underneath. As he looked, the mushroom gradually changed colour. Its brown cap became a livid flush with bright scarlet spots, and its stalk sprouted a black fringe. The mushroom smiled, a wicked, secret smile, and Daljit thought he heard it say, 'Trick and Eat.' Then the picture and the sound disappeared, and there were only the words on the card.

'I like that word, *masquerading*. It's more interesting than cats and mats and Rover and that lot.'

'There are plenty of remarkable words like that, and I will teach you them all,' Mr Jones said. But not all the cards that Daljit read that day were quite as splendid as the masquerading mushroom or the fishing flies. Before he left, he had read and copied out eleven cards and learned several new words, but he had not seen any more magic. He thought that perhaps Mr Jones was disappointed in him for refusing to come to watch a spell in the early hours of Tuesday morning.

'See you on Wednesday,' Mr Jones said, at the front door, and Daljit said, 'Yes, Mr Jones.'

'What did your aunt Sarry teach you this weekend?' Daljit asked Ben when they met at school on Monday.

'Taught me about a boy called Martin who was a spy.'

'How could he be a spy if he was a boy?'

'Stupid! No one would think of a spy being a boy, that's why they chose him.'

'What sort of spy was he?'

'Found secret plans for new bombs and planes and guns and that sort of

thing. He got to know a guy who was an inventor, and he copied his plans.'

'That's sneaky!' Daljit said, shocked.

'You have to be sneaky if you're a spy.'

'Who chose him? I mean, who wanted to know about the inventions?'

'His country did. Because this guy was inventing secret weapons, for another country, see? And they had to know about them, so they could stop this other country using them when they fought.'

'It's a bit muddling,' Daljit said.

'It isn't when my aunt Sarry reads it out to me. It's exciting.'

'What's it got to do with your learning to read?'

'It's the way my aunt Sarry teaches, see? She reads me a bit out of a book, and I have the same book, so I can see what she's reading. I'm supposed to be looking at the words while she's saying them. Does your Mr Jones read to you?'

'Not exactly. He has cards . . .'

'I know! *Cat sat on mat*, and that sort of thing.'

Daljit remembered Mr Jones's cards and said, 'His cards are different.'

'This Martin, he's a whole lot more fun than cats and mats. There's a bit where he's copying out a plan and he nearly gets caught. The inventor guy begins by being a bit suspicious, but then he thinks "They'd never put a boy on a dangerous job like that", so he stops bothering to lock everything up all the time. It's brilliant. I bet I get to read before you do,' Ben said.

Daljit thought that if Mr Jones's magic didn't last longer than a minute or two, Ben might well win his bet. He

thought that when he went back to
Elder Grove on Wednesday, he would
ask Mr Jones to try to hurry up with his
ordinary teaching or better still, do
some magic that would last longer than
a couple of minutes.

Chapter Four

But on Wednesday, Daljit did not see Mr Jones.

He went to Number 81, Elder Grove at the usual time and rang the front door bell. But no one opened the door.

After waiting a little in case Mr Jones was talking on the telephone, or in the toilet, he rang again. But still no one came.

Mr Jones must have forgotten that he was meant to be teaching Daljit that day. Daljit felt disappointed and rather hurt. He had been looking forward to hearing what had happened when Mr Jones worked his spell. And as he thought of this, a sound from the ground near his feet made him look down. He expected to see a dog, or

perhaps a cat. He certainly had not
expected to see what he did see.

For some time he just stared at the
hedgehog and the hedgehog stared back.
It had round black eyes like
blackcurrants, and it was very very
prickly.

At last, Daljit said, 'Mr Jones?' He
felt like an idiot saying this, but it did

seem too much of a coincidence (a word he was now pleased to have learned last Friday) that there should be no Mr Jones inside the house and the very animal that Mr Jones had been doing magic with, outside the door.

The hedgehog nodded. Or Daljit thought it was trying to nod. When you are hedgehog shape, with no neck between your face and your body, nodding is difficult.

'What happened, Mr Jones?' Daljit asked. But he didn't need an answer. Mr Jones had worked his spell and had turned himself into a hedgehog, but he hadn't been able to undo the spell at the right time and to become a man again.

'Never mind. Perhaps it won't last long. I'll come back on Friday and see how you are,' said Daljit, who was a kind boy.

Can hedgehogs cry? Daljit could have sworn he saw a tear glistening just below one of those curranty eyes.

He went home. There was no point in staying for a reading lesson with that sad, prickly creature. 'What did you read about today?' his Mum asked him, over tea. 'Hedgehogs,' Daljit answered, not thinking quickly enough to invent.

'Hedgehogs! Last week it was mushrooms and crocodiles. Is Mr Jones some sort of Nature freak?' his Mum asked. Daljit knew she was thinking of those clever men on the telly who explore dangerous forests and deep bat-infested caves and treacherous rivers, so that they can show us, sitting safely in our living rooms at home, the wonders of these far-off places. He could have said that Mr Jones was certainly a freak of Nature just at the moment, being a hedgehog who, a day or two ago, had been a man. But instead he said, 'He knows a lot about animals,' and left it at that. But he worried in bed that night, trying to think how he would ever be able to explain to his Mum and Dad, and worse still, to Mr Smith, that he'd had to give up his special lessons because his Tutor had turned into a hedge-pig. Ben would be reading Books long before he could, if this particular piece of magic lasted much longer.

On Friday, when he went back to Elder Grove, the door was opened as soon as he rang the bell, by Mr Jones in his own shape and in his neat blue boiler suit. Daljit didn't know whether to say anything about the hedgehog incident or not. It is difficult to ask your tutor

what it feels like, being under a spell he
himself has cast and failed to undo. But
he did think that Mr Jones's hair looked
even pricklier than it had *before* his
unfortunate experience. Perhaps that
was the bit of magic that had lasted
longest.

He said nothing about the events of last Wednesday, and tried to read the cards which Mr Jones put in front of him.

Dragons are not always dangerous.

'Aren't they? I thought they were always dangerous,' he said.

'Not if you catch them young enough,' Mr Jones said, and there, on the table between them, was a very very small, a baby dragon, not much larger than a chipolata sausage. It frisked about, investigating the pile of reading cards and Mr Jones's hand. He stroked it in an absent-minded way.

'Isn't it lovely! Couldn't I have one, too?' Daljit said. It was an enchanting little creature, with bright green scales tipped with gold, and a very red tongue which flicked in and out of its mouth as quick as a flame.

'Certainly not. Do you know how large dragons grow? How would your mother like to have a pet in her house who eats twenty pounds of meat a day? And isn't too particular what sort of meat it is,' Mr Jones added meaningly. A moment later the baby dragon had disappeared. Where it had been on the table, it had left a small puddle which Mr Jones quickly mopped up.

'Oh! I wish it hadn't gone,' Daljit said.

'I told you, my magic often doesn't last,' Mr Jones said. Perhaps he had forgotten last Tuesday and Wednesday, when his magic had certainly lasted a good deal longer than he had meant it to.

'Back to work. Read this,' Mr Jones said, producing a new card.

'*Tell me a story*. That's not very

interesting,' Daljit said.

Mr Jones said, 'Wait!' To the card, he said, 'You've been told what to do. Why don't you do it?'

'You didn't say *Please*,' the card answered in a thin, papery voice.

'Please!' Daljit said, and the card began, aloud:

'Once upon a time there were two very wicked, very clever dwarfs. One of them stole some gold and the other one used it to make a magic helmet which made the wearer invisible or let him change his shape into anything he wanted. He made a golden ring and whoever had it on his finger, had power over the whole world. But there was someone else who wanted to get the helmet and ring for himself . . .' The little crackly voice died away. Only the words, *Tell me a story* were left.

'I wanted to know what happened!' Daljit said.

'You can read about it,' Mr Jones said, and for the rest of the lesson, Daljit read out of a real book which had the story in it. Mr Jones helped him, but though he was reading about magic, there wasn't any to help him and it was hard work. He was quite pleased when it was time to go home.

'What happened to the boy your aunt's reading to you about? The one who was a spy?' he asked Ben after the next weekend.

'He found a plan about a special kind of bomb that killed people but didn't knock down buildings. It was full of bugs that give you a deadly disease that there's no cure for.'

'Is there really a bomb like that?'

'There is in this book. So he had to

copy out all sorts of numbers and things
that told what the bomb was made of,
and it took much longer than he'd
thought, and he had to stay all night in
this inventor's house.'

'Did the inventor find him?'

'No. He escaped the next morning, in a disguise.'

'What sort of disguise?'

'Got into the dustbin in one of those big paper bags. So the inventor guy carried the bin out onto the pavement, and left it for the dustmen to come round, and when he'd gone back into the house, Martin got out and went home.'

'He must've been really heavy to carry,' Daljit said.

'He could hear the guy cursing, it was such a weight. And it was stuffy inside the bag. And it smelled terrible.'

'Did you read all that yourself?' Daljit asked.

'I read some of it. Aunt Sarry reads it quite slow, so I can see the words while she's saying them. She says that's how she learned to read and she reckons I'm doing fine,' Ben said.

Daljit wished he could hurry Mr Jones up a bit. He had learned some interesting words, but he certainly hadn't been able to read much of the story about the wicked dwarf. He was in a bad mood when he went to his next lesson that Wednesday, and when Mr Jones gave him a card saying *Fasten your seat belt. No smoking*, he said crossly, 'I learned that ages ago.'

'Very well, if you're so clever, try this,' Mr Jones said.

The letters on the new card didn't make any sense at all. Daljit couldn't see a word he'd ever seen before.

'*Mansteddin ur kedishog bori . . .* What does that mean?' he asked.

'Means, "I desire the wisdom of the

ancients.''' He reached out to take the card from Daljit. But Daljit was still trying to work it out.

Very slowly, a syllable at a time, Daljit began to read it out. *'Mansteddin ur kedishog bori . . .'*

As he said the words, a curious feeling ran all over him. Bits of him seemed to be getting larger, especially his head. This bit also felt cold. His skin prickled and his clothes were suddenly uncomfortably tight. He looked at Mr Jones and thought that *he* looked different too; smaller, somehow a little foggy, and – yes, – horrified.

'Cwm cwmrie! This is something I never meant!' Mr Jones said.

'What's the matter?' Daljit asked. His voice came out not at all like his own. It was hoarse and squeaky, as if he had a bad cold.

'Oh my dear soul!' was all that
Mr Jones replied, and as he spoke, Daljit
felt something tickling his hand. He
looked down, half expecting to see one
of Mr Jones's little magic animals. But
instead of a tiny animal, he saw hair.
Grey hair. He tried to brush it away,
and found that it was fastened to his chin.

It was a beard.

'It is a horrible thing that has happened, and you must see it for yourself,' Mr Jones said. He picked up a card and spoke to it. It became a small round mirror. Mr Jones held up the mirror in front of Daljit's face, and Daljit saw reflected in it an old man with a bald head and a long grey beard. He put out a hand to send the old man away,

and the old man did the same. Then
Daljit realised that he was looking at
himself. He had become an old, old man.

'I should never have let you speak out
loud the spell that was on that card,'
Mr Jones mourned.

'But I won't stay like this, will I?'
Daljit cried.

'Of course, not, boy,' Mr Jones said.
But he did not sound very sure.

'Can't you do another spell to turn
me back into me?' Daljit asked.

'I need time to work on it. We will go
on with your lesson just now,' Mr Jones
said, and there was nothing for Daljit to
do except to agree.

But the lesson did not go well. Or
rather, it went too well. The ancients,
Daljit thought, seemed to have been
extremely wise. There was nothing they
– and now he – did not know. The

reading cards were far too easy.
Mr Jones gave him a huge book of
English poetry. He read it faster than
Mr Jones could turn the page. Mr Jones
gave him a book in German. Daljit knew
that too. Mr Jones tried him with
Greek, with French and with Welsh.
Daljit could read them all. If there had
been a book in Russian, Daljit knew that
he wouldn't have found that any more
difficult to understand. At the end of the
hour's lesson, Mr Jones was in despair.
'There's nothing I can teach you, man.
Best go back home now.'

'Do I have to go home like this?'
Daljit asked. But he knew the answer.
He had to go home. His Mum was a
worrier. If he didn't turn up this
evening, she would have first his Dad
and then the police looking for him.
He'd never be able to explain things to

his Dad, let alone the police. It would be best to have a quiet talk with his Mum first.

'Perhaps it will wear off on your way back,' was all the comfort Mr Jones could give him.

Chapter Five

As HE WALKED home, Daljit hoped that it was wearing off. Every now and then he squinted down at his beard, hoping to see it shrivel up and disappear. But it didn't. His shaky old legs felt trembly and tired, long before he was halfway home. He began to wonder whether it wouldn't have been better if Mr Jones's spell had turned him into a hedgehog too. At least that was a spell that didn't last for more than a few days.

He was trying to decide how to explain to his Mum that this was really him, Daljit, when he caught sight of Susie, who was in his class at school.

'Hi, Susie!' he said.

Susie turned away her head and didn't answer.

'Hi!' Daljit said again.

'My Mum says not to talk to strangers,' Susie said, and ran as fast as she could down the street.

Daljit walked sadly on. How could he possibly make his Mum believe that this old, old gentleman, who might have been her grandfather, was really her son?

He was passing a very small boy. The very small boy stood still and stared at him. He did more than stare. He goggled. Then he said, 'Do it again!'

'Do what?' Daljit asked.

'That what you did just then. You did look funny! Har, har!' said the very small boy.

'I didn't do anything funny. You are a very rude child,' Daljit said, quite pleased to be old enough to scold naughty little boys who laughed at him in the street. He walked away from the boy, more and more slowly, towards his own house. When he got there, he did not open the front door, although he had the key. He thought that if his Mum saw an old, old man with a long grey beard walking into her kitchen, she might faint or have a heart attack. So he rang the door bell.

When his Mum opened the door, her hands were covered with flour and she did not look pleased.

'Lost your key again?' she snapped. Daljit tried to explain.

'Don't be frightened, Mum. I know it doesn't look like me . . . There's this beard . . . and I know I'm bald, but –'

His Mum was already on her way back to the kitchen. 'Don't bother me with your nonsense. I'm in the middle of rolling out the pastry for my pie,' she was saying, not so much as looking round.

'But Mum . . . !' Daljit called, following her.

'Go and have a wash, then you can have your tea,' his Mum called back.

Daljit knew his Mum, and he went into the bathroom. First he washed his hands. Then he looked in the mirror. There he saw . . .

Daljit.

His ordinary self. No beard. No shiny bald head. Plenty of hair in the right places. He looked down and saw his own straight short legs. He wriggled with pleasure, and his clothes were comfortably loose enough for wriggling. If there'd been space enough in the bathroom, he would have turned a cartwheel for joy.

So what the very small boy must

have seen was an old bald man with a grey beard, turning back into Daljit again. No wonder he had goggled! Daljit would have goggled himself if he'd seen it.

In the kitchen, just to make sure that he was really himself again, he stole a small piece of his Mum's uncooked pastry. It was delicious. He was sure that old men with beards and shaky legs didn't enjoy uncooked pastry.

But there was still something that was different. He could feel it, but he didn't discover what it was until after his tea, when his Mum said, as she always did, 'Homework first. Telly after.' Daljit got out his school books and opened them. And, quite suddenly, he found he'd read the whole of a chapter, five pages long, without even thinking. He hadn't had to ask his Mum about one single word.

He picked up one of his Mum's magazines. In three minutes he had read two pages of small print, all about a pop star who had been married six times and was just going to have her seventh wedding. Then he started on a letter on

the back page from someone who was having trouble with a boy friend. But when he asked his Mum to explain a word he couldn't make out, she snatched the magazine away.

'But, Mum! I was reading!' he said.

She looked at the page and said, 'You were reading? How come you can read stuff like that? Last week you couldn't hardly read that spelling book you had from school.'

'Mr Jones has been teaching me real fast,' Daljit said. But he knew it wasn't just the regular teaching Mr Jones had given him with those cards that had made the difference. It was that spell about desiring the wisdom of the ancients.

He didn't feel as if he could still read German and French and Greek and Welsh as he had that afternoon while he was still an old, old man. The magic wasn't that strong. But some of it really had lasted, like Mr Jones' prickly hair. That meant that he needn't any longer be embarrassed and bored by the idea of Books. He might even get to like them. He'd be able to find out about what kept planes up in the air, and how a mustard or cress plant managed to pack all that leaf into such a tiny seed. He'd read stories for himself – and then he'd be able to tell them to his Dad instead of always being the one who listened. 'I can read better than Ben. I reckon I can read almost anything,' he said to his Mum.

'You certainly can.' His Mum was pleased, but she was still puzzled. 'That's wonderful! Your Mr Jones must be better than Ben's aunt Sarry. He must be some kind of wizard,' she said.

Daljit didn't try to explain. He just said, 'That's right, Mum. Mr Jones is as good as a wizard any day.'